Memories of Nana

Barbara Heydweiller Bull

DORRANCE
PUBLISHING CO
EST. 1920
PITTSBURGH, PENNSYLVANIA 15238

The contents of this work, including, but not limited to, the accuracy of events, people, and places depicted; opinions expressed; permission to use previously published materials included; and any advice given or actions advocated are solely the responsibility of the author, who assumes all liability for said work and indemnifies the publisher against any claims stemming from publication of the work.

All Rights Reserved
Copyright © 2017 by Barbara Heydweiller Bull

No part of this book may be reproduced or transmitted, downloaded, distributed, reverse engineered, or stored in or introduced into any information storage and retrieval system, in any form or by any means, including photocopying and recording, whether electronic or mechanical, now known or hereinafter invented without permission in writing from the publisher.

Dorrance Publishing Co
585 Alpha Drive
Suite 103
Pittsburgh, PA 15238
Visit our website at *www.dorrancebookstore.com*

ISBN: 978-1-4809-3639-3
eISBN: 978-1-4809-3662-1

I saw the look on my grandson Hayden's face when his grandfather passed away, and I realized he didn't understand that he would hold memories of him in his heart forever. I hope my book will help you hold on to memories of your special person.

I dedicate this book to my grandson Gregory. We will never get to share memories, but I will forever hold you in my heart.

Memories of Nana

My grandmother had been my best friend in the whole world. My mother told me that Nana would live on forever through all the memories we shared together. That made me feel a little better.

When I was very little, I would visit Nana at her apartment in New York City. She lived in a tiny apartment by the East River, which was far away from my house in the country. I looked forward to the visits because they were always an adventure.

Living in an apartment was different than what I was used to. Nana would store her milk on the fire escape, where it stayed cool in the chilly city air. We would spend the afternoons visiting her friends in the apartment below us. Nana and her friend would let me help them make pasta. I would lay the noodles out across the big kitchen table so that they would dry.

Some afternoons Nana would take me out into the city to explore. We would stop at the automat for lunch. Nana would let me punch the buttons on the big metal machine, and out would come a sandwich.

In the evenings, she would take me on walks down by the East River. We would stop for ice cream cones and then eat them as we looked at the bright lights from the city reflecting in the river.

Nana and I did everything together. At night, she would sit behind me with her hairbrush and carefully brush my hair. She always made sure to brush my hair one hundred times. She said it would make my hair the nicest hair around. She was right.

After living in the city, Nana decided it was time to move to the country. She came to live with my family, and I was so happy to get to spend time with her every day.

Living with my grandmother meant there was more time for us to spend together. She taught me all sorts of things, like how to iron clothes. I loved being her helper.

The best times with Nana were around the holidays. At Christmas, Nana would help me get my dolls ready for Santa's visit. We would wash their clothes and use sugar water to starch them so they were pretty and proper for Santa.

On Christmas Eve, we would dress each doll in her dress and set them out under~ neath the tree. They were ready to meet Santa, and we all hoped that he would bring them a new friend!

We also made Christmas cookies for Santa. Nana would work in the kitchen to make the cookie dough—with my help, of course. I loved sneaking cookie dough from the bowl when she wasn't looking.

On Christmas morning, I would run out to the tree to see if Santa had come and if he had brought a new friend for my dolls. I would introduce the new doll to her friends and to Nana.

Easter was another holiday that I loved spending with her. Together we would carefully dye eggs in the kitchen at the big table.

One year, Nana asked me to help her with a rinse for her hair. I was excited to get to help and listened to her tell me how to mix and apply the rinse. I worked the rinse into her hair in the bathroom as she told me stories.

When it was time to rinse the color out, Nana and I were surprised to see that her hair was bright blue! I had used too much rinse. Nana now looked like one of the Easter eggs we had colored earlier!

Even when we weren't doing hair rinses, there was something to do. Nana and I would paint our nails together in the evenings. She always wore polish that was bright red and very shiny.

I had a habit of biting my nails. One day, Nana brought home a bottle of polish that would make my nails taste bad. She hoped it would help me stop biting them.

But I loved how the polish tasted. Nana couldn't believe I was still biting my nails!

At night, Nana and my parents would sit around the table in the dining room. They liked to play cards together, and I would watch them play before bed.

While I was sleeping, she and the others would drop coins underneath the dining table.

The next morning was always a treasure hunt. I would climb under the table and look for things the adults had dropped.

Nana would watch as I carefully counted my coins and carried them back to my room. She always knew how to have fun.

Having Nana around all the time made everything better. When the family went on vacation to Florida, she would sit in the back of the car with me.

She had games for the car, just like she did at home. We played I Spy for hours. When we got tired of I Spy, we looked for different license plates on the passing cars.

We tried to find license plates from all of the different states in the country. Nana and I made up stories about the people in the cars around us and made plans for our time in Florida.

Sometimes Nana would lean over and tell me that I should drive. She was sure I could get us there faster than my father.

Even as I got older, Nana was my best friend. When I needed help convincing my mother to let me do something, Nana was there. She knew just what to say to get my mother to give in.

She and I would go shopping together. When I found a dress that I liked, she helped me hide it on the back of the rack. When we got home, Nana would tell my mother all about the dress and suggest she buy it. She was the perfect partner in crime.

Her favorite flower was the peony. She loved the way they smelled. When I grew up, I bought a painting of a peony to always remind me of her.

I have so many memories of my grand-mother and all of the great times we had together. Now it's your turn. Think about your loved one and all the fun things you share.

Use this page to write down your own memories:

_____

_____

_____

_____

_____

_____

_____

_____

_____

_____

Here's another page to share your own memories:

_____

_____

_____

_____

_____

_____

_____

_____

_____

_____

_____